There's Always Room for One More

Ingrid and Dieter Schubert

Front Street ⸷ Lemniscaat

Asheville, North Carolina

One day Beaver built a little boat just for fun.

"Look at my new boat, everyone!
Do you want to go for a ride?"

Beaver's friends laughed at his small boat.

"How can we all ride?" Bear asked. "*You* barely fit."

So Beaver built a raft big enough for all his friends.

"Do you want to go for a ride now?" Beaver asked Mole.

"Sure," Mole said as he scrambled aboard.

Then Hedgehog hopped on.

Hare swung down from the tree branch
and landed on the edge of the raft.

When Badger got on, the raft began to tilt.

The ride over the rapids was a little scary, but they
made it to smooth water without getting *too* wet.

When Bear climbed sleepily on board, the raft
sank even deeper into the water.
"Everyone off!" Beaver cried. "You're too heavy!"
"We can balance if no one moves," said Mole.

"Uh-oh!" they all cried when they
saw Butterfly headed for the raft.
Butterfly landed softly …

…and tipped the raft over!

Everyone got soaked.

And Beaver went back to his little boat.
This time he rode all by himself.